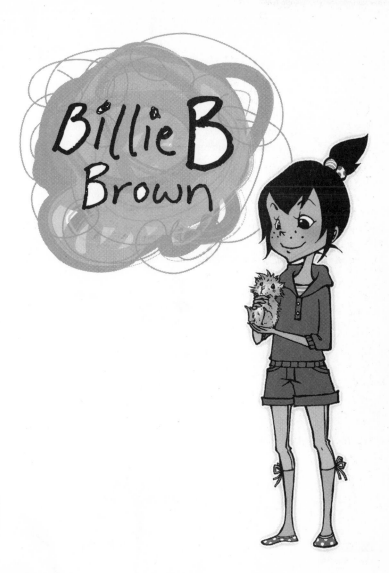

www.BillieBBrown.com

*The Cutest Pet Ever*
published in 2012 by
Hardie Grant Egmont
Ground Floor, Building 1, 658 Church Street
Richmond, Victoria 3121, Australia
www.hardiegrantegmont.com.au

A CiP record for this title is available from the National Library of Australia

Text copyright © 2012 Sally Rippin
Illustration copyright © 2012 Aki Fukuoka
Logo and design copyright © 2012 Hardie Grant Egmont

Design and typesetting by Stephanie Spartels

Printed in Australia by Griffin Press, an Accredited ISO AS/NZS
14001:2004 Environmental Management System printer.

1 3 5 7 9 10 8 6 4 2

**FSC**
www.fsc.org
**MIX**
Paper from
responsible sources
**FSC® C009448**

The paper this book is printed on is certified against
Forest Stewardship Council® Standards. Griffin Press holds
FSC chain of custody certification SGS-COC-005088. FSC
promotes environmentally responsible, socially beneficial
and economically viable management of the world's forests.

# The Cutest Pet Ever

By Sally Rippin

Illustrated by Aki Fukuoka

hardie grant EGMONT

# Chapter One

Billie B Brown has two finished puzzles, three half-read books and one broken Lego castle. Do you know what the B in Billie B Brown stands for?

# Bored.

Billie B Brown is bored, bored, bored.

Usually when Billie is bored she can play with her best friend, Jack. But Jack is away this weekend so Billie has no-one to play with.

Three half-read books

Two finished puzzles

One broken Lego castle

Billie can't even play with her baby brother Noah because he is having a nap. And anyway he is too young to play properly. He just messes up her games or tries to eat her Lego. He can be so **annoying!**

Just then Billie has an idea. A super-dooper idea.

She knows *exactly* what
she needs. A pony!

If Billie had her own
pony, she would never
be bored again.

Billie runs downstairs
to tell her dad.

Billie's dad is in the
kitchen. He is baking bread.
The kitchen is warm and
smells yummy.

'Hey, Dad,' Billie says.

'I know what I need!
A pony! If I had a pony,
I would never be bored.

If I had a pony, I would brush it and feed it and ride it every day.'

Billie's dad smiles. 'Billie, where would we keep a pony? A pony needs lots of space and lots of food. But how about a pet frog instead? I had a frog when I was a little boy. They can be lots of fun.'

Billie frowns. 'A frog?' she says. 'You can't pat a frog. A frog is a *terrible* pet.'

She **stomps** upstairs to find her mum.

# Chapter Two

Billie's mum is having

a nap with Noah.

Billie knows she is not

supposed to wake her

mum unless it is for

something very important.

But this is something very
important. She tiptoes
into the bedroom.

'Mum!' Billie whispers
into her ear. 'Guess what?'

Billie's mum opens one eye. 'Billie,' she says. 'Is this something important?'

'Very important,' says Billie seriously.

Billie's mum sighs. She turns over carefully so that she doesn't wake Noah. Then she pats the bed next to her for Billie to lie down.

Billie cuddles in next
to her mum. She is
warm and smells like
milk and flowers.

'What's up, love?' Billie's
mum asks.

'I'm bored,' says Billie.
'I need a pet to play
with. I want a pony but
Dad said no.'

Billie's mum smiles.
'What about Noah?' she
says, pointing to Billie's
baby brother. He is curled
up next to Billie's mum,
**snuffling** like a piglet.
'He's a bit like a pet.'

'Mum!' says Billie crossly.
'Don't be silly. I'm serious!'

'Sorry,' Billie's mum says.
She makes her face serious.
'Dad is right. A pony is
much too big. But how
about a pet cockatoo?
I had a pet cockatoo when
I was a little girl. I taught it
to say hello. A cockatoo
is a very good pet.'

Billie frowns. 'But you
can't cuddle a cockatoo!
What about a puppy?
Oh Mum, let's get a cute
little puppy. Please?'

'A puppy is a lot of work, Billie,' says her mum.

'I can look after it!' says Billie. 'I'll feed it and walk it and play with it every day.'

'Sorry, Billie,' says her mum. 'We are much too busy with Noah to look after a puppy right now. Maybe when he's older.'

Billie feels very **cross**.

'It's not fair!' she says loudly.

Noah wakes up and
begins to cry.

'Oh Billie!' says her mum.
'Now you've woken Noah.'

Billie scrunches up her fists and **stomps** out of the room. She is feeling very cross. It's all Noah's fault. If Noah wasn't around, Billie is sure her parents would buy her a pony *and* a puppy.

But then Billie feels bad for waking Noah.

She really does love her baby brother. Billie picks up a puppet and puts it on her hand.

'Peekaboo, Noah!' Billie says, poking the puppet out from behind the door.

Noah **squeals** with laughter. Billie and her mum laugh too.

# Chapter Three

That afternoon,
Billie and her mum go
to Westland Shopping
Centre. Billie helps
Mum put Noah into
the stroller.

He wriggles but
Billie snaps the buckles
tight. **Snap! Snap!**
Billie and her mum walk
around the shopping
centre looking in the
shop windows.

'Ooh look, the pet shop!'
Billie says. 'Can we just
take a peek? Please?'

'All right, Billie,' says
her mum, 'but quickly.
We still have lots of
shopping to do. And Noah
will need a feed soon.'

The pet shop smells like hay. All around Billie, animals **squeak** and **squawk** and **purr**. Billie sees tumbling kittens and rolling puppies and teeny tiny mice. All the pets are so cute. Billie wishes she could bring them all home with her.

Then, right at the back of the shop, she sees a cage all on its own. At first Billie thinks it is empty. But then she bends closer and spots a little round ball of ginger fur.

'Hello,' Billie calls softly. A little pink nose pokes out from all the fur.

Then two shiny black
eyes. Then two pink claws.
Can you guess what it is?
It's a guinea pig! And it's
the cutest guinea pig
Billie has ever seen.

'Mum!' Billie calls.

'Come and look at  this guinea pig. Isn't it adorable?'

Billie's mum comes over with the shopkeeper. 'She's the last one left,' the shopkeeper says. 'She's a very special guinea pig. Just waiting for a very special girl, I think.'

He winks at Billie.

Billie looks at her mum.
'Oh, please can we have
her, Mum?' she begs.
'I promise I'll look after
her and feed her every day.'

'Well…' says Billie's mum.

'Please?' begs Billie.

Just then Noah begins
to cry. He is fed up.

'Let me think about it, Billie,' her mum says. 'Come on. The guinea pig will still be here when we've finished our shopping.'

Billie squeals with **excitement**. That's *almost* a yes!

All afternoon Billie helps her mum look after Noah.

She minds him while
her mum tries on shoes.
She wipes the banana
off his hands and face.
She even passes her
mum a nappy after he
has done a stinker!

The whole time she
is helping her mum,
Billie thinks about the
guinea pig. She has
decided to call it Molly.
Billie hopes so much that
her mum will say yes!

'Thank you, Billie,' her
mum says when their
shopping is finished.

'You have been such a good helper today. I think you will be very good with a pet, too. Shall we go and get that guinea pig now?'

'Oh thank you!' Billie squeals. She jumps up and down with **excitement**. Her very own pet! Billie can't believe it. She will never be **bored** again!

Billie rushes
into the pet store.
She runs straight
up to Molly's cage.
She peers between
the bars.

But the cage is empty!

# Chapter Four

'Oh dear,' says the
shopkeeper. 'A man came
in just after you left.
He said he wanted a
pet for his daughter.
He thought a guinea pig

would be perfect for her.
I'm very sorry.'

Billie hangs her head.
*Her* Molly, gone to
another little girl? Billie
presses her lips together to
stop herself from crying.

'I'm sorry, Billie,' says her mum, giving her a cuddle. 'Shall we look for something else? Maybe there's another pet that will be just right for you.'

But Billie shakes her head **sadly**. Molly was the perfect pet. There will never be another pet like Molly.

Billie sits quietly in the car all the way home. Even Noah's noisy chattering can't cheer her up.

'I'm sure they will get some more guinea pigs at the pet shop,' says her mum.

Billie nods her head sadly.

When they get home, Billie helps carry the shopping into the house. Then she flops down on the couch. A big fat tear slides down her cheek.

She **sniffs** as she sees
her dad's car pull into
the driveway.

'Hey, Billie,' her dad calls.
'Can you help me bring
in some shopping?'

Billie gets up from
the couch and trudges
outside. Her dad is taking
a cardboard box out of
the boot. 'Here,' he says.

'Why don't you carry this inside?'

'What is it?' asks Billie.

Billie's dad smiles. 'Look inside.'

Billie peers into the box.

At first she thinks that
it is empty. But then she
sees it. A little ginger ball
of fur.

Can you guess who it is?

'Molly!' Billie shouts.

She gently picks up
her guinea pig.
Molly snuffles right
into her chest like she
remembers Billie too.

# Collect them all!

Billie B Brown
The Bad Butterfly
By Sally Rippin
1

Billie B Brown
The Soccer Star
By Sally Rippin
2

Billie B Brown
The Second-best Friend
By Sally Rippin
3

Billie B Brown
The Midnight Feast
By Sally Rippin
4

Billie B Brown
The Beautiful Haircut
By Sally Rippin
5

Billie B Brown
The Extra-special Helper
By Sally Rippin
6

Billie B Brown
The Secret Message
By Sally Rippin
7

Billie B Brown
The Big Sister
By Sally Rippin
8

Billie B Brown
The Birthday Mix-up
By Sally Rippin
9

Billie B Brown
The Little Lie
By Sally Rippin
10

Billie B Brown
The Best Project
By Sally Rippin
11

Billie B Brown
The Spotty Holiday
By Sally Rippin
12

Billie B Brown
The Cutest Pet Ever
By Sally Rippin
13

Billie B Brown
The Pocket Money Blues
By Sally Rippin
14

Billie B Brown
The Copycat Kid
By Sally Rippin
15

Billie B Brown
The Perfect Present
By Sally Rippin
★